SHOWER LAND

BREAK THE CURSE

BOOKS BY NAT AMOORE

Secrets of a Schoolyard Millionaire
The Power of Positive Pranking
The Right Way to Rock

We Run Tomorrow

Shower Land: Break the Curse
Shower Land: Feel the Freeze (June 2024)
Shower Land: Walk the Plank (September 2024)

SHOWER LAND

BREAK THE CURSE

NAT AMOORE

JAMES HART

PUFFIN BOOKS

UK | USA | Canada | Ireland | Australia
India | New Zealand | South Africa | China

Penguin Random House Australia

Penguin Random House Australia is part of the Penguin Random House group of companies whose addresses can be found at global.penguinrandomhouse.com.

First published by Puffin Books, an imprint of
Penguin Random House Australia Pty Ltd, in 2024

Cover design by Rebecca King © Penguin Random House Australia Pty Ltd
Internal design and typesetting by Midland Typesetters, Australia

Printed and bound in Australia by Griffin Press, an accredited ISO AS/NZS 14001 Environmental Management Systems printer

NATIONAL LIBRARY OF AUSTRALIA

A catalogue record for this book is available from the National Library of Australia

MIX
Paper | Supporting responsible forestry
FSC www.fsc.org FSC® C018684

ISBN 978 1 76134 252 3

penguin.com.au

We at Penguin Random House Australia acknowledge that Aboriginal and Torres Strait Islander peoples are the Traditional Custodians and the first storytellers of the lands on which we live and work. We honour Aboriginal and Torres Strait Islander peoples' continuous connection to Country, waters, skies and communities. We celebrate Aboriginal and Torres Strait Islander stories, traditions and living cultures; and we pay our respects to Elders past and present.

For Murray. Because everyone needs a book just for them – #allthesingledads

Chapter 1

That little snotrag

'**Felix** Anthony McKillop, if you don't get out of bed and get in the shower right this second, I'll …'

Felix knew better than to wait for the end of that sentence.

'Coming, Dad,' he yelled as he dragged his body out from under the warm doona and sat on the edge of his bed.

Felix raised his fingers to his eyes and prised his lids open. Mondays were always so, so hard. He dug his fingertips into the corners of his eyes and wrenched out huge clusters of crusty sleep.

Mr Claverotte, the old French guy who owned the bakery in town, had told him that in French they call it '*caca des yeux*', which translates as 'eye-poo'. As Felix wiped the yellow chunks on the underside of his bedspread, he decided that was a pretty good name for it.

'FELIX!'

'I'm up!'

Felix's pyjamas were all twisted, and the bottoms had risen way past where it was okay to wear your pants. He yanked them down and straightened his t-shirt. His hair stuck up in different directions, but he couldn't blame that on just waking up. Felix's hair always looked like he had just woken up. It was very uncooperative.

As he tried to pat it flat, his bedroom door burst open and his little brother, Olly, ran in.

'Dad says if he doesn't hear the shower running in one minute, he's gonna send you to school in the jumper Granny gave you for Christmas,' Olly jeered, happy to be the one delivering this threat.

He then pulled out his favourite thing in the world – his copy of *Biggest Book of Best Jokes, Insults & Comebacks.*

Super-catchy title.

Felix rolled his eyes at Olly. There were only two years between them, but he felt like his eight-year-old brother was from another planet.

'You're so hairy, you went to a dog show ... and won!' Olly cracked himself up.

'That's not funny, Olly. It's also not true.' Felix checked his top lip every morning, hoping for signs of a first moustache hair. So far, nothing!

Olly glared at him. 'You wouldn't know funny if it leapt out of the toilet and bit you on the butt.'

Felix tried to straighten the doona on his bed enough that it could pass for 'made'.

'Well, I know what isn't funny. And it's ***that*** book. It's so juvenile.'

'What's juvenile?'

'It means it's immature stuff that only little kids find funny.'

'Immature, huh?' Olly flicked through his book. 'Well ...' He landed on a page. 'Immature is just a word boring people use to describe fun people.' Olly threw his head back and snorted with laughter. 'See? I'm calling you boring. Take that!'

Felix shook his head and stood up, pushing past Olly. 'Move it, butt-face.' He shoved his younger brother aside and headed down the hall towards the bathroom.

'**Butt-face**, huh? Well ...' Olly flicked through his book again. 'Why do ducks have tail feathers?'

Olly was like the ads you can't skip on YouTube – there was no escaping him. Felix walked into the bathroom and shut the door in Olly's face, but it didn't stop him.

'To cover their **BUTT-QUACK**!'

'Go away, Olly, I'm having a shower!' Felix yelled through the closed door.

'Oh, you *should* have a shower . . . 'cos your armpits smell so bad your teacher gave you an A-plus for not raising your hand.'

It was useless trying to make him stop. Olly had been testing his jokes on Felix for weeks now, ever since he found that annoying book in the local second-hand bookshop. Olly thought they were hilarious, but what does an eight-year-old know about what is funny? Epic fail videos on YouTube are funny. #AnimalsActingLikeHumans is funny. POV memes are soooooo funny. Olly's joke book is just **NOT**.

Maybe a nice shower would wash away the frustration of having to start every day with the world's most unfunny stand-up comedy routine. But somehow, Felix doubted it. He stripped off his clothes, trying to block out the annoying voice behind the door.

'Hey, Felix, you're as much use as a chocolate teapot. Get it? 'Cos it would just melt?'

Felix stepped into the shower, keen for the sound of water to drown out his brother's insults.

'Ooooh, this one is perfect for you because you are *such* a bad dancer,' Olly started.

'I wish I could just get away from that little snotrag,' Felix muttered as he turned on the tap, and water shot from the showerhead.

'What do you call a dancing sheep?'

Felix never heard Olly's punchline.

The water hit his head and . . .

REEEEKKKKKK!

There was a sound like rusty brakes on a metro train, a blinding flash of white light and the strong smell of singed hair.

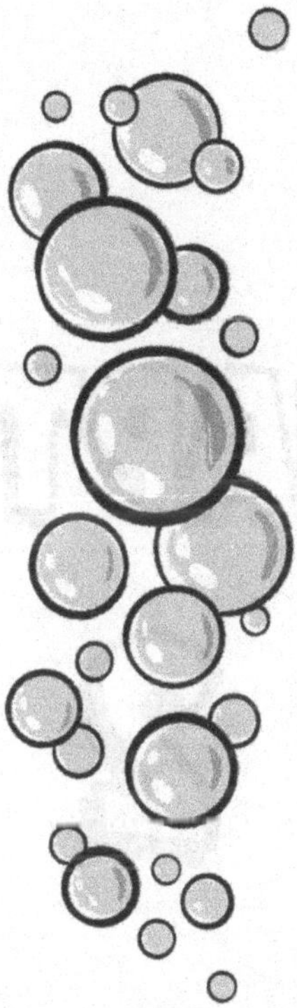

CHAPTER 2

Naked and desperate

Whaaaaattt?!?!?!

Felix felt grass prickle beneath his feet.

Wait! Was he ... outside?

A cool breeze made him glance down.

'Aaaarrrgghhh!'

Felix was as naked as the moment he stepped into the shower. Both his hands dived down to cover his bits. He searched for answers to the thousand questions that whirled through his mind. And also, for a pair of pants!

He was standing in the middle of a large field and he had no idea where he was or how he got there.

'Attack!'

The cry came from behind Felix, and he spun around.

Soldiers ran over the top of the ridge and down the hill towards him. An army! Some were on foot brandishing swords and carrying shields, some had bows and arrows drawn and others were on horses with long spears under their arms.

'Raaaaarrrrr!'

From the other direction a pack of villagers rushed towards them. They were dressed in olden-day clothing, carrying sticks and pitchforks and a bunch of other random weaponry.

And Felix was in the middle.

Naked.

He spotted a blue-and-yellow shield lying on the ground and grabbed it. Holding it over the bits that mattered, he bolted out of the way.

Just in time too! The two groups collided in an explosion of clanks and crashes and bad words.

Felix ran.

Up ahead, just beyond the field, was a small farmhouse. With no other option, he headed for it, leaving the battle behind in a cloud of dust.

It was a smart choice. There, in the front yard, was a clothes line, full of clean washing. Felix would not normally take something that wasn't his, but desperate times called for desperate measures. And being naked in a strange land counted as **VERY** desperate times.

Felix checked that the coast was clear.

Music wafted from the house, but he couldn't see anyone. He paused for a moment to listen. Was it a violin? It wasn't being played like the painful performances at the end-of-year School Spectacular (which was absolutely

NOT spectacular!). This violin was full of joy, and the music bounced along, almost making Felix want to dance.

But Felix was still naked. And naked was no time to dance.

He threw the shield over a small wall surrounding the farmhouse and climbed over. On the other side, he picked the shield back up and looked around the paved courtyard. It was a small place, just like where he lived, but instead of blue weatherboard, this house was made of a wooden frame, filled with clay walls and a thatched straw roof. It looked like the houses in the Robin Hood movie they'd watched at his friend's birthday party.

But it was probably more important that Felix focused on clothing himself than admiring the architecture, so he tiptoed past a small chicken coop and over to the clothes line.

The brick paving was warm under his feet and the clothes on the line waved at Felix invitingly as they flapped in the wind. At home, Felix had a Hills hoist in the backyard. He and Olly had broken it about ten times by using it as a swing, so it was held together with rope and gaffer tape. This one was just some twine strung between two thick bits of timber. There were different pieces of clothing hanging along the line. To Felix's relief, at one end there was a pair of brown pants and a simple white shirt that would fit him perfectly.

'Burk!' A chicken clucked at him disapprovingly.

'Don't look at me like that,' Felix whispered. 'I'm just borrowing them.'

The chicken cocked its head to the side and gurgled deeply. **'Beeeeerrrrk.'**

'What would you know, birdbrain?' Felix said, pushing the guilty feeling down. The chicken looked hurt. 'I didn't mean that. Sorry. I'm sure your brain is ... just fine.'

Why was he talking to a chicken? He really *had* lost his grip on reality. As well as all his clothes!

Felix dropped the shield again and plucked the pants off the line. Quickly slipping his legs into the pants, he grabbed the shirt too, then froze.

BUSTED!

CHAPTER 3

Not real

There, next to the house, stood a boy about his age with curly red hair and an unimpressed look on his face. He crossed his arms and raised an eyebrow at Felix. His face clearly said, 'Excuse me?

Are you right there? Hanging around naked in our backyard and stealing clothes from our line?' You know when one look can say **ALL** of the things? Well, this look did that.

'I, um, I'm really sorry. I was . . . you see, I was having a shower, and then . . . and I had no clothes . . . and the soldiers . . . and . . .' Felix was getting nowhere fast.

The boy's hands moved to his hips.

'Look, I'm really sorry about the clothes, it's just I was naked and **desperate**. I can give them back . . .' Felix dropped the shirt and moved his hands to the buttons of the pants, preparing to take them off and return them to the boy.

The boy's eyes widened as he shook his head, covered his eyes and waved a hand at Felix.

Felix stopped. Taking this as permission, he grabbed the shirt from the ground and threw it over his head.

The boy peeked from between his fingers to check that Felix was still clothed. Frowning at him, he pointed, indicating that Felix should stay where he was, and then disappeared into the house. The bouncy violin music stopped, and the boy came back, pulling along a girl the same age and with the same fiery red hair as his.

'What, Noah? What do you . . .' The girl stopped when she saw Felix. 'Oh.'

The boy pointed his finger accusingly at Felix and then turned back to the girl.

'Wait, Noah, are they your clothes?' she asked, staring at Felix's outfit.

The boy nodded furiously.

Felix felt his face go red. 'Yes, look, I'm really sorry. It's just I was having a shower and then I was here and I had no clothes …'

'Whooooooooooa!' The girl's eyes widened as she looked at the shield on the ground next to Felix. 'Is that a Devonfield soldier's shield? A real one?'

Felix looked at the shield and shrugged. 'I guess?'

'Ha! Let's make a trade. I keep that and you can keep the clothes. I've got some old boots you can take too.'

Noah didn't look impressed at her willingness to give away his clothes and boots.

But Felix couldn't knock back free clothes right now. **'Deal!'** he agreed.

The girl rushed up and grabbed the shield. She turned it over, inspecting every part and running her fingers gently across the raised emblem on the front. She stuck her hand out to Felix.

'I'm Elsie,' she said with a grin that scrunched up all the freckles on her face.

Felix smiled at Elsie and shook her hand.

'And that's my twin brother, Noah.'

Noah folded his arms across his chest, still unimpressed. He did *not* smile.

'I'm Felix. And sorry again about the clothes. And thanks!'

'Not a problem!' replied Elsie. 'I'll get a good trade for this shield. It's in great nick.'

Felix turned to Noah. 'Sorry if I scared you, Noah. Sneaking over the fence and all.'

Noah continued to glare at Felix.

'Ah, so maybe you're a little angry with me?' Felix looked himself up and down, realising he was dressed head to toe in Noah's clothes, which had been given away entirely without his permission. 'Oooohhh, is it okay? That she gave me these?'

Noah shrugged and then gave a small nod.

Felix cocked his head to the side. 'Do you not talk?'

Noah shook his head.

'Is it –' Before Felix could ask Noah his question, Elsie jumped in, talking over the top.

'He's never talked. Ever. Some people think it's because he doesn't like them but that's not it.'

'How do you know? Maybe it's also that he doesn't like me.' Felix turned back to Noah. 'I mean, I haven't got things off to a great start with you, have I? Stealing your clothes and trespassing in your backyard? Not exactly how all good friendships start.'

Noah gave Felix a small smirk then looked to Elsie and wiped it off his face.

'Can I ask why you don't speak?' Felix didn't want to be rude, but he also wanted to understand. But Elsie jumped in again.

'Oh, a witch put a curse on him when he was a baby and stole his voice,' explained Elsie.

Felix **burst** out laughing.

The two siblings stared back at him.

Elsie furrowed her brow. 'Not exactly what I'd call funny.'

Noah's eyes widened and he looked at Felix like he'd just **burped** at the Queen's dinner table.

Felix glanced between them. 'But you can't be serious?' His smile faded. 'There's no such thing as witches and curses.'

'Is that so?' Elsie raised her eyebrows. 'Maybe you should explain that to Noah, who has spent his life never able to say a word? I'm sure he'd be happy to hear that it's all not real.'

On top of his disbelief in witches' curses, Felix felt a little weird about the way Elsie kept talking about Noah like he wasn't there. And what was the big deal if Noah didn't talk? Did something need to be to blame?

Felix asked Noah, 'You don't think you have a witch's curse, do you?'

Noah shot a quick look to Elsie then raised an eyebrow at Felix, who swallowed hard and let his eyes drop to his feet.

Maybe he didn't know enough about this world. He felt like he was stuck in one of those old-fashioned fairytales.

Elsie smiled. 'There you go! So where are you from that you don't have witches' curses?'

Felix sighed. Elsie had a good point. There were plenty of things Felix needed to rethink. Like magic showers and teleporting to other lands and red-headed boys with witches' curses.

'But how do you know it was a witch's curse?' Felix asked.

'A very **reliable** source told me.'

Noah slapped his thighs and threw his hands in the air.

Felix smiled. Noah clearly didn't agree that Elsie's so-called reliable source was very reliable. This made Felix feel better about his doubts.

But Elsie ignored him. 'We always knew there had to be a reason and now we know, it's a witch's curse.'

Felix had read enough outdated fairytales to know what his next question should be. He looked to Noah apologetically as he felt ridiculous for even asking it. But Felix stepped up to the mythical plate.

'Is there a way to break the curse?'

Noah covered his eyes and shook his head and Felix could read him perfectly. That head shake said, '**Oh no**, not another one.'

CHAPTER
4

Home sweet home

'The only way to break the curse is by making him laugh,' Elsie explained.

'Well, that's easy!' Felix said and, with that, he turned to Noah, crossed his eyes, pulled on his ears and stuck out his tongue. Noah just stared at him, unimpressed. Felix stopped, feeling a little silly.

'It always works on my brother Olly,' he said quietly.

'Yes, well, growing up with a curse on you tends to kill your sense of humour,' said Elsie.

Felix glared at Elsie. 'I doubt his sense of humour is the issue. Maybe I'm just not that funny.'

Noah tilted his head towards Felix. He seemed intrigued by the new boy's take on things.

'What do you find funny, Noah?'

'Nothing,' Elsie answered.

Felix glared at her. 'I was asking Noah.'

Noah's eyes darted between the two of them then he shrugged and shook his head.

'See!' Elsie said. 'Nothing.'

Felix thought about it. 'Wow, that must suck.'

'Suck?' Elsie questioned.

'Um.' Felix searched for another word. 'It must be hard for you.'

'He's used to it,' Elsie said with a shrug.

Noah's eye roll suggested the thing that might suck the most for him was a sister who always steamrolled the conversation.

But Felix decided it wasn't his place to get in the middle of whatever this family dynamic was.

He looked at the house instead. It was small, but cosy. It felt like a home. It reminded him a little of their house in Cork Bay. He wondered what his dad was doing right now. Was he worried about his missing son?

'Where are your parents?' Felix asked. 'Are they going to be angry that you gave me these clothes?'

Elsie's face dropped. 'They're not around any more. It's just us.'

'You mean you live alone? And take care of yourselves?'

Elsie looked at him, confused. 'We *are* ten years old. It's not like we're children. Noah starts his first job next harvest.'

Felix tried to imagine Olly and him getting by without their dad. Felix couldn't even get Olly to flush the toilet, let alone take care of himself AND get a job. 'Wow. That's **amazing**.'

Noah scoffed.

'Or it's not?' Felix questioned, unsure.

'Not really,' Elsie explained. 'It means he has to go away. All we want is to stay together, but the money we get from the chicken eggs is not enough to live on. And we don't want to lose Ma and Pa's house. It's all we have left of them.'

'And you can't go too?' asked Felix.

Elsie shook her head. 'They are only hiring boys, which is completely ridiculous. Everyone knows I work way harder than Noah.'

She looked at Noah, who shrugged in agreement.

Felix shuffled his feet in the dirt. 'Okay, well ... thanks for the clothes.'

Elsie grinned at him. 'Hey, we were about to head to the town fair. You want to come with us?'

Felix's mind raced. He didn't know what to do. He felt like he should try to find a way home, but he also didn't want to be alone. He was more confused than the time he'd lost his dad at Luna Park. 'I think I should try to get home. Dad will be seriously flipping out that I've disappeared.'

Elsie shrugged. 'Okay, then. Where's home?'

Felix looked around, unsure. He pointed in the direction he came from. 'Over there, I think.'

Elsie scoffed. 'Well, the farmers are fighting again so I wouldn't head in that direction for a few hours. You might get impaled by a **pitchfork**.'

Felix laughed.

Elsie looked at him, confused. 'It wouldn't be the first time it's happened.'

Felix stopped laughing. It suddenly dawned on him – he didn't know where he was ... or how he got here ... OR how to get home. And he was in a place where people could get caught in the crossfire of **flying pitchforks**! He maybe, just a little, felt like ... not crying ... but a bit like he might have something in his eye.

Elsie put her arm around Felix's shoulder. 'Don't worry. We can help you find your way home.' She looked over to where Felix had pointed. 'That's west, so maybe you're from Hadleigh?'

Felix shook his head.

'Breckenshire?'

'No.'

'Ailsforth! You could definitely be Ailsforth kin.'

'What does that mean?'

Elsie smiled. 'Ailsforth folk are just … different.'

Felix wiped his eyes. 'I'm from Cork Bay.'

Elsie shook her head. 'Never heard of it.'

Felix looked around and down at the clothes he was in. He knew he was further away from home than he could ever explain to Elsie. 'I don't think it's near here,' he said quietly. 'And I don't know if I can ever get back.'

'Nonsense!' stated Elsie. 'There is always an answer to everything.' Elsie suddenly grabbed Felix's arm, hard! Her eyes widened as her fingernails dug into his skin. 'That's it!'

She grinned wildly and Noah began to wave his hands in the air and shake his head furiously.

But Elsie nodded. 'Oh yes! We're taking him to see **Mystical Mago**.'

Felix heard a slap and turned to see Noah's head in his hand. He assumed it was a ye-olde-time facepalm.

'Who is Mystical Mago?' Felix asked nervously.

Noah ran his finger over his palm, then waved his hands wildly in the air.

'Don't start with that!' said Elsie. 'The fortune teller knows exactly what he is talking about.'

Felix was confused. 'Wait, what fortune teller?'

'That's how we found out about Noah's curse,' explained Elsie. 'Mystical Mago told me that's how Noah lost his voice *and* how he can get it back.'

Excitedly, she squeezed Felix's shoulders in what felt like a WWE move. 'We can take you to see the fortune teller and find out how to get you home. It's **genius**,' cried Elsie. 'Which is why I thought of it. Now, do you have any money?'

Felix raised an eyebrow at her. 'Um, I don't even have clothes. Where do you think I might be hiding money?'

'Good point. Don't worry, we can use the egg money. I'll fetch you those boots. Let's get packed and head into town.'

Felix followed Elsie inside.

Noah trailed behind, shaking his head.

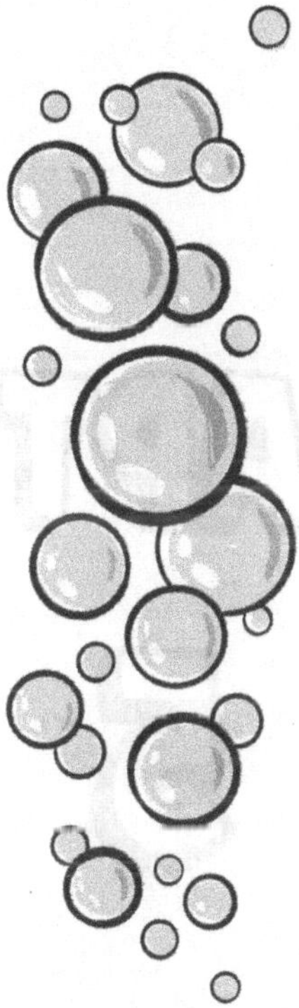

CHAPTER 5

No Ubers here

Next thing Felix knew, Elsie was dragging him out the door and down the road. At least he was now wearing boots.

Noah walked behind them, lugging a large woven basket full of eggs that Elsie had packed up to sell. They had been delicately laid on a nest of fabric to be carried into town. Felix was impressed with the size and number of the eggs. His neighbour, Ms Caras, had a chicken, but it laid about one egg a month if she was lucky. And it was barely half the size of these. Felix regretted insulting the chicken. It was clearly very good at its job.

'Here, you carry this,' Elsie said, shoving the shield Felix had found into his arms. 'We should be able to trade it in town.' Felix took the leather strap of the shield and slung it across his shoulder, wearing it like a backpack.

'We'll drop the eggs off to Agnes to sell,' Elsie explained, 'then take you to Mystical

Mago and then check out the town fair because ... well, it's the town fair and no one misses the town fair. And *then* we can help you find your way home. What an exciting day. Ready for an **adventure**, Felix?'

Felix thought maybe he had had enough adventures for one day, but he didn't have any other plans and he didn't want to be alone. Elsie seemed nice and Noah ... well ... Noah looked like he might put up with Felix tagging along if he gave his best puppy dog eyes.

Noah shrugged a 'whatever' at him.

That was good enough for Felix.

'Okay. Thanks, Elsie. Thanks, Noah.' He felt better about things already. At least there was a plan. A plan that put chicken

eggs before his safe return home. But a plan nonetheless.

'So, this town fair, what's it like?' Felix asked.

Elsie's face lit up. 'Oh, it's wonderful. There are fortune tellers, musicians, dancing, dragon rides and, of course,' she turned and looked directly at Noah, **'JESTERS!'**

Noah sighed and shook his head.

Felix looked between them, trying his best to accept the fact that 'dragon rides' was on that list. 'What's wrong with jesters?'

Noah shook his finger, then held his belly and pretended to laugh.

'Not funny?' Felix asked.

Noah pointed at him and tapped his nose.

'Only **you** don't find them funny!' Elsie scoffed and turned back to Felix. 'I've been taking him to see them for years to try to break the curse, but Noah's the only person in town who doesn't think they're funny. It's like he doesn't even *want* to break the curse.'

Felix glanced over at Noah, who made a beak with his hand and mouthed **'blah blah blah'** as he moved it like a talking puppet. Felix tried to stifle a laugh. It must be annoying for Noah, always having Elsie talk for him. Felix felt his pain. If anyone had annoying-sibling compassion, it was him.

Noah gave him a sideways smile while Elsie barely drew breath.

'But Mago told me the only way to get his voice back is to laugh, so I don't care what it takes. Even if I have to take him to every jester in the land, one day I'm going to …'

Elsie continued chatting away as Felix took in his surroundings. Had he time travelled? He didn't remember being taught about an era with witches' curses and dragon rides in history class. Was it another world? Another planet? **Another dimension?** Felix's head swam with the possibilities, and he felt a little sick. He stared at his feet, trying to concentrate on something that felt familiar, something he understood. He understood walking. Walking was the same here as it was at home.

The dusty dirt road reminded Felix of the path to the beach near his place during summer. The ground looked thirsty and puffs of dust surrounded his foot with every step.

The boots Elsie had given him weren't a perfect fit so they rubbed a bit on his heel, but he wasn't going to complain. Dad had made him wear 'dress shoes' to his auntie's wedding. Shiny, stiff black shoes that made every single toe feel like it was being squished in a juice press. These boots were nowhere near that bad.

Felix kind of liked how heavy they felt. They made him walk with purpose.

CLOMP. CLOMP.

Going to find a way home.

CLOMP. CLOMP.

Going to figure this out.

CLOMP. CLOMP.

Going to avoid getting eaten by a dragon or impaled by a pitchfork.

'You sound like one of the Great Horses!' Elsie laughed. 'Maybe you could carry us to town?'

'Or we could just call an **Uber**,' Felix joked.

Elsie and Noah gave each other side-eyes.

'Right.' Felix nodded. 'No Ubers here.'

Elsie began to step in time with Felix. 'It sounds like a strange land, this . . . Cork Bay . . . that you come from.' She grinned at him. 'I would love to travel, see more of the country. Of the world. Can you tell us about your village?'

Felix looked up at the huge trees that lined the path. They were nothing like the eucalypts back home. These trees had thick strong trunks, and branches that snaked off in every direction. Each branch was full of thick clumps of green leaves and they seemed to come alive with every breath of wind.

'It's very, **very** different to here,' Felix explained carefully. 'It might be hard for you to believe.'

Elsie shoved him gently. 'I believe in witches' curses. Try me.'

Noah nodded, pointing to himself and giving a thumbs up, which Felix took as, 'Try me too.'

Felix told them about home. About wagons that didn't need horses, that took you from place to place in five times the speed. About giant metal birds that carried people between countries. About lights that operated without fire, at the flick of a switch. And about metal devices that allowed you to talk to people anywhere in the world and watch TikTok videos.

Both the siblings' eyes got wider and wider as Felix talked. He worried that their heads might explode.

'Wait, what is a **TikTok**?' Elsie asked, her 347th question in the last ten minutes.

Felix was exhausted trying to explain his entire world. 'Your turn, tell me everything about you two. Have you always lived here? What do you do every day?'

Elsie seemed happy to explain their world to Felix. She talked and talked and talked, chatting away like she barely needed to breathe in between sentences. Felix thought Olly was a lot, but Elsie could definitely do with an off switch. She was very kind, but Felix would have loved to get to know Noah better.

As Elsie talked, Felix looked at Noah. He had a nice face that was very expressive and right now it said, 'Here she goes again.' Felix caught his eye and Noah smiled. He spread his arms like he was holding a balloon then did his puppet again. Then repeated the balloon action, followed by making a heart with his hands. Elsie was still chatting away, oblivious to the silent conversation going on behind her.

'Big mouth, but big heart?' Felix whispered.

Noah grinned and winked at him, his freckles scrunching up as he did so.

Felix wondered if it was hard for Noah, not being able to talk. Or if it was just hard having a twin who talked **SO** much. He imagined what Noah's laugh would sound like. Not because it would break some kind of curse, but because he would bet a golden chicken egg it sounded **great!**

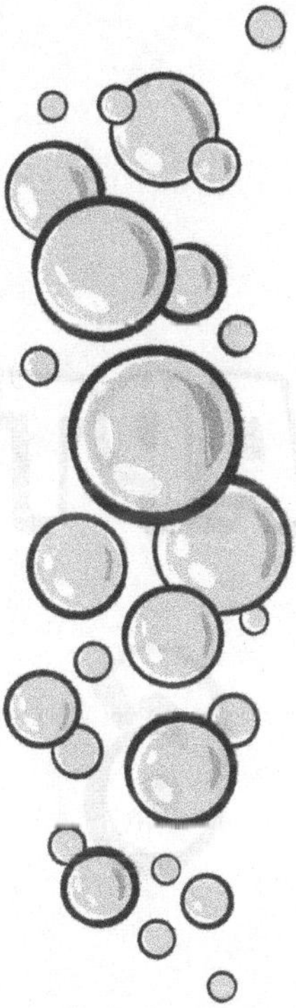

CHAPTER
6

It's a . . . it's a . . . dragon!

The kids passed a pond where a family of ducks played in the water, diving below the surface and shaking the water off their feathers. Felix stopped to watch them for a second, wishing he had some bread to feed them. Then something moved in the field behind the pond. Long stalks filled the field and, as he stared at them, they rustled again. There was definitely something moving within. He walked along the pond edge to peer through the tall brush.

'Aaaarrrghhh!'

Felix leapt into the air and stumbled backwards, tripping and landing on his butt. There, just beyond the pond, was a dragon! A real, living and breathing, legit dragon. He pointed at it and yelled to the others.

'It's a ... a ... look, it's a ...' Felix couldn't get the words out.

'I think the word you are looking for is **dragon**?' Elsie said indifferently. She was as surprised by the dragon as someone in Cork Bay might be by seeing a bin chicken.

The dragon wasn't very big, maybe the size of a large pig, and was kind of round.

Its yellow and orange scales shimmered in the sun and two bull-like horns poked out from its head. Sitting on its hind legs, it clutched a cob of corn between its front claws. Sharp teeth munched at a high speed as it slid the cob back and forth, rotating it slightly each time and removing every single kernel of corn. When finished, it held the cob by one end, dangled it overhead, opened its mouth wide and dropped it inside, swallowing the cob whole.

'They are such a pest,' Elsie complained. 'Eating crops and pooping on our roofs. Nothing worse than **dragon poop** in your chimney.'

The dragon lifted its head at the accusation and looked Felix directly in the eye. Felix slowly crept backwards, whispering to Elsie.

'It's not going to **eat me**, is it?'

Elsie laughed loudly, startling the dragon. 'A corn gobbler? Eat you? Hardly! Strict vegetarians, those ones. But try keeping them away from your compost!'

'Are you sure?' Felix was unconvinced. From what he'd read in books (mostly fantasy, granted, but it seemed relevant right now), dragons could be pretty dangerous.

'Absolutely. Nothing to worry about. But if you see one of the blue and red ones, then run for your life. They are not called **bone suckers** to be cute.'

Felix backed up towards the path, refusing to take his eyes off the creature. The dragon reached for another corncob. As it used its teeth to peel back the husk, the little hairy husk bits tickled its nose.

AAACHOOOOOO!

The dragon sneezed, blasting a stream of fire from its nostrils onto the corn. The corn started to pop.

Pop! Pop! Pop! Just like it did in the microwave when Olly, Felix and his dad had movie nights back home.

The sound scared the dragon and it jumped up and ran to the other side of the field, quickly turning its attention to a new juicy corncob.

Noah was way ahead by now, with Elsie not far behind.

'Hurry up, Felix,' Elsie yelled back to him. 'The town is still an hour away.'

An hour!? Of walking? Felix really wished Uber was a thing in this place. He chased after the siblings, slowing to follow behind them. His mind was blown. He had just seen an **ACTUAL** dragon. Where was he? Every second he spent in this place he felt another light year away from his little blue weatherboard house in Cork Bay.

He tried to focus on walking again, to push down the panic attack that was threatening to rise in his chest. He stared at Elsie's back and concentrated on what was in front of him.

'What's that?' Felix asked, pointing to the leather case that bounced on Elsie's back as she walked.

Elsie reached behind and gave the case a loving pat. 'That's my fiddle.'

Noah shrugged an imaginary fiddle case up on to his shoulder and then circled a finger around his head.

Elsie smiled. 'Yes, it goes with me

everywhere. What can I say? It's my prized possession. And my best friend.'

Noah let a look of shock and hurt pass over his face as he pulled out his invisible heart and broke it in two.

Elsie's laugh filled the air. 'Don't worry, Noah, you're a pretty close second.'

'Ah, yeah. I think I heard you playing back at the house?'

Elsie spun around, her face bright red. 'You heard that?'

'Um, yeah.' Felix paused. 'You are **really good**.'

Elsie squirmed uncomfortably.

'Maybe you could play a bit more for me?' he asked. 'I haven't heard anyone play that well before. Fasi at my school plays, but it sounds more like a Tasmanian Devil with a squeaky toy stuck in its throat.'

'Like a what?'

'Never mind. Can you play me some?' Felix begged.

'No way!' Elsie said furiously. 'I don't play in front of people. **Ever!**'

'But you're so good.'

'Never!' she yelled and marched off down the road.

Noah shrugged and jogged to catch up to her. Felix sped up, not wanting to be left behind just in case there was one of those bone suckers around. They didn't sound like much fun.

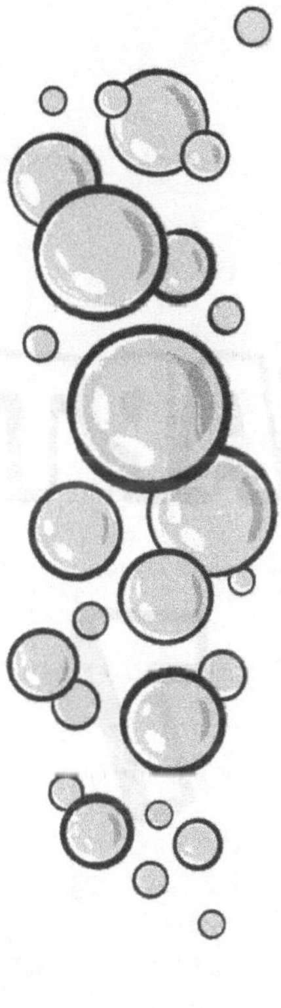

CHAPTER 7

Hand-knitted socks

Felix could hear the town before he could see it. He could smell it too! It smelt like animals. Lots of animals. As he walked up over the peak of the hill, he saw the dirt path lead into a bustling town square. They stepped through the entrance, revealing a cobbled path lined with market stalls, people selling food from the backs of their wagons, crates of chickens and pens of goats. There was even a cage with a small corn gobbler inside.

Felix eyed off the trapped dragon. 'Can't it, like, burn its way out?'

Elsie patted him on the back. 'Don't worry, you're safe. Their fire breathing doesn't work when they are captured. Strange quirk of nature.'

Felix remembered seeing a polar bear at the zoo who walked around in a figure eight and tapped the glass two times with his paw on every round. Animals aren't

themselves in captivity. It was sad. And so was this dragon ... scary as it might be.

The town was alive with people and animals and chatting and music. Stallholders shouted about their latest special, and food lay out in the midday sun. It was noisy and it was smelly. And it was one of the coolest things Felix had ever seen.

'It's like a **movie!**' he said.

'What is a moo-vee?' asked Elsie, sounding the word out like she had peanut butter stuck to the roof of her mouth.

'Oh, um, it's a thing we have back home. For entertainment. Like a story to watch where people play out parts,' Felix tried to explain.

'This Cork Bay county you are from is a strange place,' said Elsie. 'We just call that a play.'

Felix smiled. 'Yeah, that's it. Sort of.'

Noah raised the basket of eggs he was holding and pointed to a nearby market stall. A young woman in a cream dress with a blue apron over the top waved to them from behind a table covered in fresh vegetables.

Elsie nodded. 'Thanks, Noah. I can never get as good a price from Agnes as you do.' Noah huffed into his hand and ran it smoothly through his hair. 'Sure, sure, the silent charm,' Elsie scoffed. 'Well, please go and use it over there.' Noah smiled and disappeared into the crowd.

He returned with an empty basket and a small pouch jingling with coins.

Elsie held out her hand. 'Thank you,' she said forcefully.

Noah clung to the coin pouch, glaring at his sister.

Elsie's hand didn't move. 'Unless you know a better way to get Felix home, we are taking him to see **Mago!**'

Noah breathed deeply and reluctantly handed over the pouch.

Felix could hear music coming from the town centre and desperately wanted to head into the middle of the action. But that was not on the cards. Elsie grabbed his arm and dragged him towards a worn red velvet tent set up on the right-hand side near the town wall.

Noah trailed behind, clearly unimpressed.

A sign out the front read:

The Mysterious World of Mystical Mago – Fortune telling, card reading, potions, remedies, curse removals and hand-knitted socks

'Hand-knitted socks?' Felix queried.

'It's just a side-trade that he does,' Elsie explained. 'Don't worry, answers are his main business.' She pulled Felix towards the tent. 'Let's find out how to get you home.'

Another hand grabbed Felix's right arm. Noah pulled in the other direction, shaking his head. Elsie turned on her brother.

'What, Noah?'

Noah shook his hand in front of his face then rubbed his finger and thumb together, throwing something invisible into the air and glaring at his sister.

'It is not a **waste of money!**' Elsie said. 'Mago knows what he's talking about. He helped you, didn't he?'

Noah shook his head furiously, but Elsie just yanked on Felix. And with that, he slipped out of Noah's grip and disappeared into the darkness of the tent.

Felix's eyes slowly adjusted to the low light inside. At a round table in the centre sat a small man with a strange gold hat. A green robe was tied under his neck and a glass ball balanced on a brass stand in front of him. The tent was lit by dozens of candles, which Felix couldn't help but think were quite the fire hazard. Incense burned, trinkets and stones hung from the roof and there was a general sort of Halloween kids' party vibe.

'Welcome to the magical world of Mystical Mago,' the man boomed, raising his hands to the sky. 'Enter if you dare! Discover what secrets your future may hold and where the forces of the past may guide you. Seek answers to questions

held deep in your mind or perhaps purchase a potion to solve your woes.' He waved his hands over the ball and muttered some words that Felix didn't understand. His dad did that all the time when he stepped on one of Olly's Lego pieces.

Mago then threw his hands towards Felix and stared at him from under his bushy eyebrows. 'I sense you seek answers.'

Elsie squeezed Felix in excitement. 'He does, Mago! He **DOES** seek answers.'

The man then dramatically pressed the sides of his head and closed his eyes. 'You are trying to find something. Something important.'

'Yes!' squealed Elsie.

'A person. A person of great importance.'

'Not really,' said Felix. 'A place. I'm trying to get home.'

Mago glared at him. 'But at your home, is there not a person of great importance?'

Felix shrugged. 'I mean, my dad, I guess.'

'See! Mago is never wrong. I see all … for the small price of two silver coins.'

The tent shook, and they turned to see Noah at the entrance tugging angrily on the tent's fabric. He frowned and held up one finger.

'We thought it was one coin,' said Elsie.

Mago huffed. 'Yes, well, the cost of the foreseeable future has gone up. It's now two. BUT the new price does include ...' Mago reached down behind him and pulled out a pair of socks that looked like they'd been knitted by Olly. Who *cannot* knit. '... a free pair of **handcrafted feet warmers.**'

Elsie shrugged. 'That seems like a fair trade.' She snatched the socks and threw them at Noah. Handing over two silver coins, she pushed Felix down into the seat opposite the fortune teller.

Mago rubbed the glass ball in front of him and stared deep into its reflection. 'It's answers that you seek. You need to find your way home. A path but to where you belong.'

Felix looked at Elsie. She looked hypnotised by the man. Felix not so much.

'Um, yeah, we just told you that,' he said.

Mago glared at him and shouted, 'You do not need to tell Mystical Mago anything! **He knows all.**'

Felix was getting a bit tired of the man's theatrics. It reminded him of Olly when Felix changed the Netflix show he was watching. Sooooo much drama.

'Okay,' said Felix. 'Well, what I really want to know is how do I get home?'

'I know you want to know that!' Mago shouted. 'I told you! I know everything. I even know what you want to know.'

Felix wondered if Mago knew how annoying he was.

The fortune teller rubbed his ball once again and gazed at the nothingness.

'Every problem has a solution. The solution you seek may not be to the problem you must solve. Find the problem and solve it to receive the solution you seek.'

Felix stared at the man. 'Huh?'

Mago whipped his cape over his shoulder. 'That is all. Mystical Mago has given you the answers you seek and now **you must go!**' He leant back in his chair, dramatically raising the back of his hand to his forehead. 'Mago needs his rest.'

The tent shook. Felix and Elsie looked to Noah, who growled and beckoned with his hand.

Felix turned to Elsie. 'I think he wants the money back.'

'No refunds!' Mago announced as he jumped to his feet and shuffled the children out of his tent. He pushed them outside, spun a sign around to read **CLOSED** and sealed the tent behind them.

'Well, that was a waste of time,' said Felix.

Noah raised his eyebrows and stared directly at Elsie with a look that clearly said, 'I told you so.' Felix had given Olly this same look many, many times.

'No, it wasn't,' Elsie stated confidently. 'We know everything we need to know to get you home.'

Felix and Noah stared at Elsie, mouths agape. Felix wondered if the incense in the tent had gone to her head.

'Um, and what exactly did we learn?' asked Felix.

Elsie placed her hands on her hips. 'Well, obviously you have to solve a problem to get home. Mago made that pretty clear.'

'He did?'

'He did!' Elsie elbowed Felix in the ribs and gestured towards Noah. 'Now, all we have to do is find you a problem to solve.'

Felix's mouth fell open like a character in a Bugs Bunny cartoon. Did she just call her brother '*a problem to solve*'?! Felix called Olly a fart-sandwich once and got no screens for a week but even that seemed less offensive.

Noah rolled his eyes and pointed to his ears.

Felix turned on Elsie. 'I think he's trying to tell you that he can hear you talking about him.'

'I know that!' She glared at her brother. 'But Noah is a **PERFECT** problem for you to solve. Make him laugh, lift the curse, he can speak, you go home, happily ever after.'

That was about all Felix could handle. 'Maybe he doesn't need to speak. You can speak and all you seem to do with the skill is say some pretty outrageous and inappropriate things about your brother!'

Felix could feel himself getting fired up. He turned on Noah. 'Doesn't this make you mad?' Noah glanced between his sister and this new kid. He looked like he had something he wanted to express but then stopped, shrugged and walked away.

'See!' Elsie stated.

With that, she grabbed Felix's arm and dragged him into the village and towards the bustle of the town square.

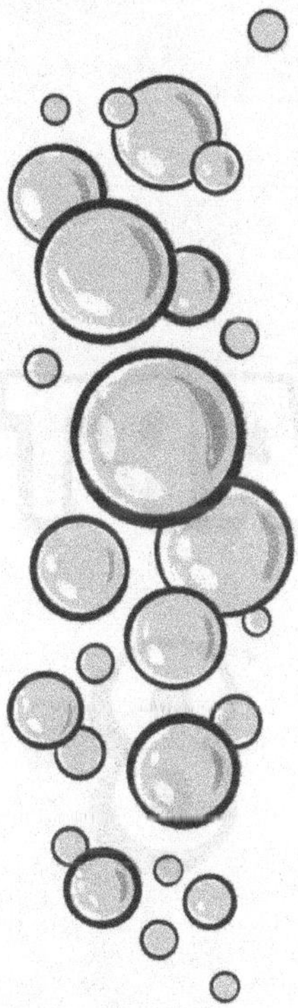

CHAPTER 8

Splat!

Since Felix had been here … wherever 'here' was … he had been dragged around a lot. Like, **A LOT**.

He didn't know much about what had happened to him or why, but he knew he wanted to go home. And, at the moment, the only clue he had on how to get there was what Elsie had suggested.

Find a problem. And solve it.

Felix turned to Noah. He didn't really look like someone who needed help. Especially Felix's help. And to refer to Noah as 'a problem' made Felix feel uncomfortable in all sorts of ways. But Noah hadn't argued and if Felix was ever going to see his dad (and yes, even Olly) again, he would have to give it a shot.

He would make Noah laugh and break his curse. A weird feeling crawled up Felix's spine. Like when he was reading one of those books written **AGES** ago where all the baddies were described using words we would **NEVER** say these days. But these weren't 'these days', were they? And maybe Felix had to do things this way to get home. Even if it made him **VERY** uncomfortable.

Felix didn't think he was especially funny. But he knew what *was* funny. Unlike Olly. He thought of the epic fail videos that always cracked him up. The classic one where the Canadian guy keeps slipping on ice and falls over for thirteen minutes straight. People falling on their butts was funny, for sure. He would give that a try.

There were plenty of people and animals in the town square for the fair. Up ahead, a horse had kindly left a large wet poo on the footpath. It was clearly a fresh one as steam was still rising from it in the crisp spring air. Felix turned to Elsie and started talking, deliberately 'not watching' where he was going.

'I don't know how I got here. I mean, one second I was in my bathroom and the next second I . . .' With that, Felix plonked his boot directly in the pile of horse poo and let it slide. His feet flung up in front of him and his body fell backwards.

SPLAT!

Felix landed hard with his butt right in the middle of the horse dung.

'*Ba ha ha ha!*' Elsie exploded with laughter.

That was a good start, but she wasn't the intended audience. Felix looked up

hopefully at Noah. He just stared down at him, his fingers pinching his nose to block out the stench. But not even a smile.

Elsie reached down and helped Felix back to his feet, wiping tears of laughter from her eyes. 'Oh, that was great! Did you see that, Noah?' she said.

Noah nodded, tossed Felix an old cloth from his pocket and continued walking.

'That boy has zero sense of humour,' said Elsie. 'That was **hilarious!** Are you okay?'

Felix nodded and used the cloth to wipe the horse poo off his butt. He watched Noah walk off. So, hurting himself didn't work. It did, however, leave him smelling like poop.

'Here, you missed a bit.' Elsie grabbed the cloth and tried to wipe the mess out of Felix's hair, but instead it kind of matted into it.

Despite now having poo-hair, Felix hadn't even managed to get Noah to crack a smile, let alone laugh. So, what else was funny? Felix thought of all the time he spent watching prank videos on YouTube.

Practical jokes were funny! Playing a trick on someone. That always gets people cracking up. Felix played pranks on Olly all the time. One time, he put tape over the sensor on the TV remote and almost wet himself laughing at Olly trying to change the channel. Another time, he put a couple of drops of green food dye in the bottom of Olly's cereal bowl. When he filled it with milk, it turned green and he thought his breakfast was mouldy. Felix had laughed heaps at those pranks, so he was sure a good practical joke would get Noah giggling.

Felix looked between Noah and Elsie. Everyone knows a prank is funnier when it's played on someone else. Olly once got Felix with a rubber spider on his pillow and it wasn't nearly as funny as when Felix watched pranks happening to *other* people.

'Why are you looking at me like that?' asked Elsie.

'No reason,' Felix lied. He felt bad that Elsie would be the target, but he only knew two people in this whole town . . . in this whole world, actually, and he needed to get Noah laughing. So, Elsie it was. Now he just had to think of a practical joke.

As they walked through town, they passed a huge chestnut tree. Chestnut cases lay scattered around the base of the tree and had started to dry out. They looked a lot like **spiders**, which gave Felix a great idea. He secretly bent down and picked up a case, sliding it into his pocket. Pretending to look at some flowers being sold at one of the market stalls, he dropped behind the other two.

Then, quietly creeping up behind Elsie, he gently placed the case in Elsie's hair.

It clung to her curls perfectly, looking exactly like a big black spider.

Waiting a beat, Felix then shouted in his most dramatic voice: 'Elsie! There's a **spider in your hair!**'

Elsie spun around. 'What? Where?'

'There!' Felix pointed. 'Near your right shoulder!'

In one ninja-like move, Elsie reached around calmly, grabbed the chestnut case, threw it to the ground and stomped on it, crushing it to pieces.

Felix just stood there with his mouth open. There had been no high-pitched screams. No dancing around like her pants were on fire. No wild swiping at her own head while screaming at everyone around to **'GET IT OFF!'** It was nothing like when Olly had done it to Felix.

Elsie was completely unfazed.

'Aren't you scared of spiders?' Felix was stunned.

Elsie looked at him strangely. 'Why would I be scared of a little spider?'

Felix suddenly felt very self-conscious. 'Um, 'cos they are scary.'

Elsie laughed. '**Scary?** Those cute things? Hardly. Fire-breathing, bone sucker dragons are scary. Angry swamp orcs are scary. Famine is scary. Armies terrorising villages and burning them to the ground are scary. Spiders are . . . kind of cute.'

Felix felt even more ridiculous than he had ten seconds earlier, if that was possible.

'Plus –' Elsie kicked the chestnut case with her foot '– that wasn't even a spider.' She looked up and her eyes widened. 'Wait, did you put that on me? Were you trying to scare me? And you thought **THAT** would work?' Elsie cracked up laughing, her wild giggles bouncing around the town square. 'You know last year I entered the battle arena against a river troll? And you thought a tiny spider was going to scare me – **BA HA!**'

So, Felix discovered level three of feeling ridiculous was also possible. He hung his head and snuck a look at Noah, who just seemed over the whole thing and a little embarrassed for Felix.

Elsie slapped Felix on the back. 'You are a very strange person, Felix.'

CHAPTER 9

Not the problem

Music wove its way through the people crowding into the town square. Elsie turned her head towards the sound. 'The musicians are playing. I'm heading over. Pass me the shield, Felix. I'm going to trade it for some butter and bread. Keep looking around if you like, but try not to get into too much trouble, spider man.'

As Felix ducked his head out of the leather strap across his chest, he didn't bother trying to explain that where he came from, being called Spider-man was actually a compliment. He passed Elsie the shield and, as she patted him on the head and walked away, Felix knew very well that it was not meant as a compliment.

Noah didn't look too happy about being stuck with the weird kid who kept trying and failing to make him laugh.

Felix thought about giving up, but what if the fortune teller was right?

What if the only way to get home was to solve the problem? Felix couldn't give up, no matter how ridiculous he felt. Why was it so hard to make Noah laugh?

Olly laughed at almost everything Felix did. He would give anything to hear Olly's laugh. The way it went all high-pitched and then he started **snorting** when he really lost control. Felix felt so homesick, he'd even love to hear one of Olly's annoying jokes right now.

'Why did the scarecrow win a prize?' Felix said to himself, thinking about how Olly bounced from foot to foot when he told a joke he was excited about.

Noah looked up, eyebrows raised, but Felix barely noticed.

'Because he was outstanding in his field.'

Felix had hoped the joke would make him feel a little better, but it just made him miss home even more.

'Pfft.'

What was that? Felix lifted his head. He looked at Noah, whose lips were pressed together tightly and curled ever so slightly at the ends.

Was he ... **smiling?**

Almost laughing?

Felix stared at Noah as he clenched his jaw. He totally looked like he was trying to stop himself from laughing. Like Felix and the other kids did at school when Mr Baird bent over to check the

HDMI connection on the smart screen and flashed them all his butt crack.

Was it Olly's joke? And why would Noah be trying **NOT** to laugh?

'What do you call an elephant that doesn't matter?'

Noah held his face still, refusing to react.

'An irrelephant.'

Noah cracked. His lips curled up at the side and his shoulders lunged forward as a laugh escaped his mouth.

Felix couldn't believe it. Olly's jokes! *They* were the key to making Noah laugh!

'What does a garlic do when it's hot?'

Noah shook his head at Felix, grinning wildly.

'It takes its cloves off.'

Noah burst out laughing, doubling over and grabbing his stomach, eyes watering.

'BA HA HA HA!'

Felix grinned, watching as Noah laughed until he was out of steam and had finally collected himself. Noah stood up straight, a look of relief crossed his face and he smiled at Felix.

'I can't believe that worked!' Felix shouted with excitement. '**I did it!** I broke the spell. I got your voice back. Say something! Maybe "thank you" would be a good start.'

Felix eagerly waited for him to answer, but the smile slipped from Noah's face.

'What?' said Felix. 'Go on. Talk. There's no spell any more.'

Noah looked around, then grabbed Felix's hand, pulling him towards a building in the corner of town.

'Where are we going?' Felix yelled. **'Answer me, Noah.'**

But he didn't. He just kept dragging.

A beautiful old building sat before them, and Noah pulled Felix inside. The walls were lined with books and scrolls. Ladders reached up to shelves so tall you could barely see them. It looked like something out of the *Beauty and the Beast* movie.

'Noah! What are we doing here? Let's go find Elsie and tell her we **broke the curse!**'

Noah raised his finger to his lips. He pointed to a sign on the wall. Written in old-timey calligraphy, it read ***Please be quiet***. The entire library was empty except for a small man who sat at a big desk, reading.

The man looked up as Noah came in and gave him a little nod before returning to his book.

Noah continued to the back corner, where a stack of paper sat on a table with a quill resting in an inkwell. When they reached the paper, Noah released Felix's hand and picked up the quill.

He scratched something quickly on the paper in front of him, then pointed at it for Felix to read. It said:

Can you read?

Felix laughed. 'Of course I can read. I'm ten.'

Noah frowned and scribbled something down. Felix leant over to see.

Elsie is ten and she cannot read.

'Oh.' Felix dropped his head in shame. He was lucky enough to go to school, but he also had a dad and didn't have to get a job at ten years old, so maybe he should check himself a little. 'That was rude. Sorry, Noah.'

Noah shrugged and continued to write.

I don't speak. That's it. It has nothing to do with some ridiculous witch's curse. Elsie wants to 'fix me'. But I don't need 'fixing'. I've laughed before. Nothing changes. This is who I am.

Felix finished reading and looked up at Noah. 'Have you told Elsie? Because she seems super-convinced by this witch's curse thing.'

Noah put the quill back to the paper.

I tried, in the beginning. But she seems to NEED to believe it. So I let her go. But I'm perfectly happy. She's the one who's not.

'What do you mean?' asked Felix.

Noah rolled his eyes and turned back to the paper.

Where to start? She's so busy worrying about me, she forgets to worry about her own life. When I start work next harvest, I don't even know what she's going to do. She needs to focus on herself and leave me alone.

'Yeah, you don't strike me as someone who needs help,' said Felix. 'Which is great for you, but doesn't **help me get home**.'

I wouldn't trust a thing that comes out of Mystical Mago's mouth.

Felix nodded. From his limited experience, Mago's mouth did seem to produce a whole lot of **nothing!**

The problem was, he didn't have anything else to go on. If breaking Noah's curse wasn't going to get him home, what was? He was glad Noah was happy, but now Felix was back to square one.

If square one was in another world.

Don't worry, Noah scribbled down on the paper. *We'll figure something out. Come on, let's go enjoy the show.*

CHAPTER 10

Taste sensation

The boys left the library, Noah giving the librarian a quick wave on the way out. They made their way back into the town square. Felix was expecting the fun-filled celebrations that had been warming up earlier, but instead the square was filled with a group of farmers waving their pitchforks and yelling at town guards.

'You need to do **something** about it!' screamed one man.

'We will go out of business,' yelled a woman.

'This is why we pay our taxes!'

Noah squeezed Felix's hand and pointed through the crowd. He could spot Elsie's hair bobbing up and down, and they snaked their way towards her.

'Hail there!' Elsie yelled, spotting them through the crowd. 'Where have you two been?'

Felix took the lead on this one and put his hand gently on Noah's shoulder. 'Just getting to know each other a little better.' Noah smiled and took the basket from Elsie. Inside was the bread and butter that she had traded for the shield.

Felix felt good that he had at least contributed *something* to their household, even if it was by accident. 'What's going on here?'

'The farmers are fighting **AGAIN!** It's supposed to be time for the music, but they have crashed the fair, demanding help from the army.'

The farmers thrust their tools in the air, chanting, 'Help save our corn, **help save our corn!**'

Felix looked at Elsie, confused. 'Save the corn from what?'

Elsie sighed. 'From the corn gobblers, of course! This has been going on all year. The farmers want help controlling the pests, the army say they have better things to do, so they spend all their time fighting while nothing is getting fixed. Innocent bystanders are getting hit by stray pitchforks and we can't enjoy anything nice without it being interrupted by **THIS!**' Elsie waved her hand towards the fight brewing in the town square.

The farmers formed a semicircle in front of the army. A few of them dragged a cage into the circle, and Felix recognised the dragon inside as a corn gobbler.

It looked like it might be a baby one and the poor thing looked terrified. On the other side, farmers held stalks of corn and chanted loudly …

'Corn can't survive with gobblers alive!'

'It's us or them!'

'Destroy the pest, for corn at its best!'

The farmers started poking at the baby dragon through the bars of the cage. Felix was no dragon fan, he was terrified of them. But he also couldn't stand to see any animal, even one that might possibly bite his head off, be treated badly. He wouldn't even let Olly squish a daddy-long-legs, but he also made somebody else take it out into the garden.

'What are they doing to that poor dragon?'

Elsie looked at him confused. 'Poor dragon? They are a **pest!**'

'Says who?'

'They eat the farmers' crops. And if the farmers don't have crops, they can't sell them. Then their families will go hungry.'

Felix understood what Elsie was saying, but he couldn't bear to watch the little creature be harmed. Puppies at his local shelter had been mistreated in their past and it broke Felix's heart. Dragons were pretty much just scaly puppies. Who could fly. And breathe fire. It didn't matter. They were living creatures and they needed help.

Maybe **THIS** was Felix's mission. Maybe if he saved the dragon, he would be sent home. Where puppies were fluffy.

He ran between the people in the crowd and into the middle of the

Felix snatched a corncob out of a farmer's hand and peeled back the husk. He swiped a leather hat from another farmer and grabbed the knife he held. Felix scraped the corn kernels off into the hat. Walking over to the dragon's cage, Felix took a deep breath and unlatched the door.

'What are you doing?' shouted a farmer.

But Felix ignored him. He had to help the little creature.

'It's just a scaly puppy,' Felix whispered to himself. 'It's just a scaly puppy.'

The dragon looked up at him with big yellow eyes, and Felix could see it was more scared than he was. He relaxed a bit and coaxed the dragon out. 'C'mon, little one. I won't hurt you, I promise.'

The yellow dragon sniffed his hand and slowly and cautiously stepped out of the cage. Felix leant down with the corn husk and tickled the dragon's nose. Its snout twitched and, as it sneezed, Felix held up the hat full of corn to the flames.

The corn was heated.

And it began to pop.

Pop! Pop! Pop!

The delicious smell filled the air as the crowd watched in amazement.

Felix waved to his friends. 'Elsie, Noah! Bring me some of that butter.'

They ran over, and Felix scooped up a slab of butter, laying it over the hat full of popcorn. Mouths watered as the crowd watched it melt over the white puffs.

'Now,' Felix said, a smile spreading across his face. **'Try it!'**

He passed the hat around the crowd, each person taking a butter-soaked piece of popcorn and dropping it into their mouths. Eyes widened, lips were licked and tummies grumbled for more.

'It's delicious.'

'Delightful.'

'A taste sensation.'

'I want more!'

'I'd pay twice the price for corn like this.'

'What do you call it?'

Felix popped a piece into his mouth. 'I like to call it "popcorn".'

Everyone stopped and stared at him. 'Well, that's a ridiculous name,' said one of the farmers. 'We shall call it **"butter-covered-gobbler-corn puff balls"**.'

Felix smiled. 'That works too.'

The farmers patted each other on the back for their genius product-naming skills and shoved more corn puff balls into their mouths.

'Now, you should know,' Felix announced, 'I have, um, spoken to the dragon and, er, it has been made very clear to me that corn puff production only works when the dragons are **free**.' The dragon raised an eyebrow at Felix. 'So there shall be no more cages. Or else there will be no more … corn puff balls.'

It wasn't Felix's finest or most eloquent moment, but the farmers seemed to buy it.

'Very well, we can agree to that.' A farmer stuck his hand out to shake with Felix. 'No more cages, plenty more puffs. You have our word, wise corn-gobbler whisperer!'

Felix shook the farmer's hand, then the man faced the crowd. 'Three cheers for the corn gobblers!'

HOORAH! HOORAH! HOORAH!

The head of the army gave Felix a thankful smile. 'Now, can we return to the day's festivities?'

'Yes!' said the farmer. 'And we will be selling butter-covered-gobbler-corn puff

balls just over there. Only one silver coin per hat full.'

Felix hoped they would find a more hygienic way to serve their snack, but for now it would have to do.

'Excellent! Let the music begin.'

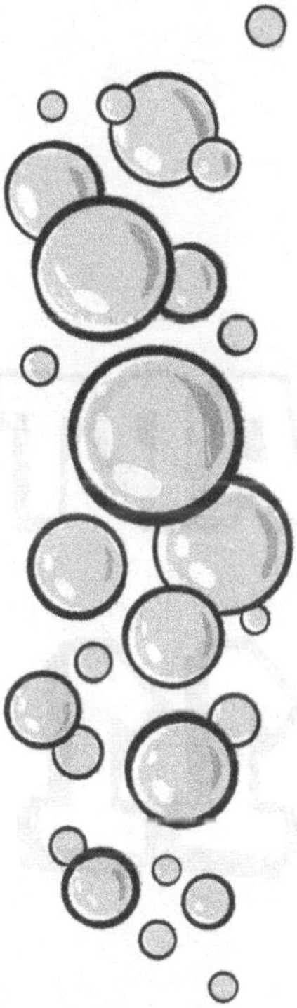

CHAPTER 11

Nothing to lose

The farmers disbanded and the town square filled with people, their attention focused on a small stage in the centre. Three drummers, dressed in red-and-black robes, played as the beat echoed through the crowd. Toes everywhere tapped along.

Elsie's face lit up. 'Yes! Back to Open Stage Day.'

'What's that?' asked Felix.

'Only the best day of the month.' Elsie bounced with excitement. 'Anyone can perform. See that line of instruments over there? You just add yours to the line and when your turn comes, you get up and perform.'

'Awesome!' Felix grinned. 'So go put your fiddle there.'

Elsie spun around, a look of horror passing across her face. '**Me?** Play in front of ... people? Not if my life depended on it.'

'Wait, what?' Felix was confused. He'd heard her play at the house and she was amazing. He'd seen kids get up on stage with less talent than a cement-filled goldfish. 'Why would you not play? **You're great!**'

Elsie shook her head furiously. Noah coughed and drew a square in front of him, and then made a screaming face. He looked a lot like the kid from *Home Alone*, but Felix guessed that reference would go over their heads, considering movies didn't even exist here.

'Um, she has stage fright?' Felix asked.

Noah nodded.

'It's not stage fright!' Elsie folded her arms. 'I'm not scared of the **stage**,

I'm scared of all the people *around* the stage, looking at me, with their **beady little eyes**.'

Felix laughed. 'Right. So you have beady little eyes fright?'

'Exactly.'

'Well, what if you closed your eyes?'

Felix suggested. 'Then you wouldn't know they were looking at you?'

Elsie leant towards Felix. 'I can still **FEEL** them looking at me,' she whispered.

This was actually pretty fair. Sometimes Felix could feel his dad's eyes on him even before he knew he was there. Mostly when he was doing something wrong.

Stage fright was also something Felix could sympathise with. One time his teacher made him be a dancing tree in the school production. He'd made such a fool of himself that by the second night the teacher had suggested he just be a 'really still tree'.

Felix felt a tug on his pants and looked down to see a little girl standing next to him.

'Are you the kid who slipped over bottom first into the horse poo?' she asked.

Great! After all the good he had done in this strange land, **THAT** was how he was going to be remembered. 'Um, yeah, that was me.'

'Ha!' she laughed. 'That was hilarious. You must be so embarrassed!' And with that she walked off.

Ouch! That was a bit harsh. But at the same time, Felix didn't know anyone here, so what did he care? It was hard to worry about people laughing at you when you didn't know any of them.

He froze. **That's it!**

'Elsie! What if no one was watching you while you played?'

Elsie furrowed her brow. 'What are you talking about? You have to play up on that stage there. In the middle of the square. The *entire* town is looking at you!'

'Do you trust me?' asked Felix.

Elsie threw her hands into the air. 'I barely know you.'

'Yeah right, fair enough. But you can trust me.' Felix turned to Noah. **'Can't she?'**

Noah held his stare and finally nodded to his sister.

Felix took Elsie's fiddle and went to lay it in line with the others.

'Don't worry, I know what I'm doing.'

Elsie looked unconvinced. She stood there shaking slightly as the other musicians got up one by one and her fiddle crept closer and closer to the front.

Finally, it was her turn.

'You've got this, Elsie,' Felix whispered to her as he gently pushed her towards the front. 'Trust me, no one will be looking at you.'

Elsie stepped up onto the stage and Felix went with her, standing by her side.

'You can do it,' he assured her. She nervously pulled her fiddle out of its case. Felix watched as her hands trembled. She slowly rested the instrument on her shoulder, glancing down at Noah, who stood at the foot of the stage. He put a fist to his chest and pointed to her. Felix was pretty sure that meant, 'You've got this.'

Elsie stared at the audience in front of her. Her eyes widened and she leant towards Felix. 'Um, Felix, they are **ALL** looking at me. There's no way I can do this.'

'Just start playing.' Felix squeezed her arm. 'Once you start playing, no one will be looking at you, I promise.'

Elsie shook her head but took a deep breath. She closed her eyes and drew the bow across the strings.

A toe-tapping melody bounced from the fiddle and filled the air. Felix took a deep breath too and whispered to himself.

'No one knows you, you've got nothing to lose.' He ignored the little voice that replied 'except your self-respect' and he started to dance.

If that's what you could call it.

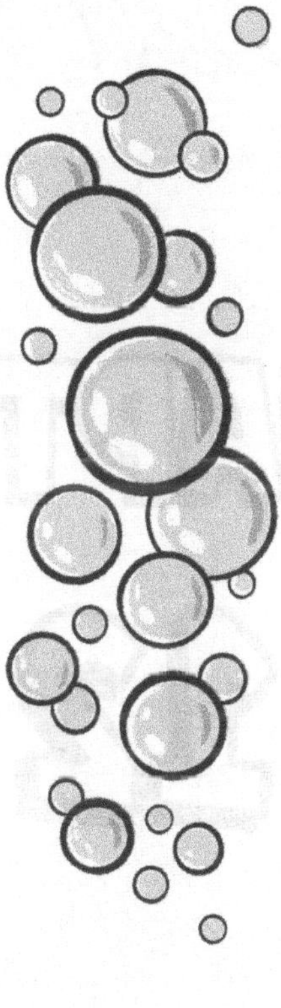

CHAPTER 12

Broken egg beater

When Felix danced, he looked like a wobbling jellyfish ... who had been electrocuted ... wearing rollerblades ... on slime. So, you know, not exactly graceful. Felix's arms and legs moved in opposite directions like they had never even met each other before. His head snaked from side to side like his neck was struggling to keep it attached.

And **EVERYBODY** was looking at him.

Noah burst out laughing.

Elsie didn't notice. She could see everybody was focused on Felix's bizarre dance routine and realised there were no eyes on her. Her chest puffed up and a grin spread across her face.

She picked up the pace and launched into a double-time tune.

Felix tried to keep up. His arms and legs flailed around like a broken egg beater, and the audience **cheered**.

Noah looked around, beaming with pride at his sister entertaining such a huge crowd. He jumped up onto the stage and joined Felix.

Felix could tell Noah was quite a good dancer. His moves started off coordinated and were actually on-beat. Felix shook his head though. That's not what Elsie needed. She needed distraction. Good old awkward, ridiculous-looking, orangutan-style distraction.

'Less "smooth moves" and more "baby giraffe learning to walk"!' Felix yelled at Noah. 'Like this!' He did his best impression of an octopus being attacked by bees.

Noah received the message loud and clear and followed Felix's lead. He threw away his natural rhythm and quickly started to resemble someone whose limbs were all broken and who had been thrown into a milk churner.

Nailed it! That's exactly what Felix's dancing looked like.

With Felix and Noah flailing about on stage, no one was looking at Elsie, but they certainly were *hearing* her. The crowd cheered and clapped along and, one by one, they also started to dance. One lady looked like a squid caught in a ceiling fan. A young man resembled a rag doll in a blender. And one kid looked like a lemur walking on hot coals.

It was **weird**.

And it was **wonderful**.

When Elsie's song finally came to an end, everybody stopped. Arms stopped swinging, legs stopped thrashing and a quiet fell over the crowd. But only for a second ...

'Woooohooooo!'

They erupted in applause.

Noah and Felix stood still, panting and grinning,

Elsie's mouth dropped wide open as she heard the crowd cheering for her. 'I did it,' she said. 'Thanks to you, Felix, I did it. No one was looking at me and I did it.'

Felix smiled. 'And they loved it!'

Elsie gave him a big hug. 'Thank you. Thank you so much.' She pulled Noah into the hug. 'You too, brother.'

Felix, squished between the siblings, made a suggestion. 'You might want to take a bow.'

Elsie released the boys and they gently nudged her forwards. She smiled

at the audience, held her fiddle to the side and took a bow. The crowd went wild. She then called the boys to her side and they held hands and all took a bow together. The crowd went double **wild**.

After taking in all the adulation, the threesome stepped down off the stage.

'That was **incredible**,' Elsie gushed. 'I never thought I could do that, play in front of people. But I did it, thanks to you, Felix.'

'Not only me.' Felix shoulder-bumped Noah. 'This guy has some pretty sweet moves too.'

Noah laughed, and Elsie joined in, then stopped suddenly. 'Wait! Noah, did you just laugh?'

Noah looked at Felix. He turned back to his sister and nodded slowly.

Elsie jumped up and down. '***Eeekkk***, that means you can talk! Say something!' Noah shook his head and Elsie stopped bouncing. 'But . . .'

Noah tapped his lips and shrugged with a smile.

'You're fine with not being able to talk?' Elsie said.

Noah nodded. He then laughed, pointed between them and drew his fingers together.

Elsie shook her head. 'But you want to be able to laugh with me? I don't understand.'

Noah nudged Felix and nodded towards his sister.

Felix explained: 'There's no witch's curse, Elsie. Noah hasn't laughed because he hasn't wanted to disappoint you when you found out that it wouldn't break the curse. But he misses laughing with you. He doesn't need to change. He needs you to be okay with him just the way he is.'

Noah put his arm around his sister and gave her a squeeze, raising his eyebrows in a look that said, 'Okay?'

Elsie laughed. 'Of course. I only want you to be happy.'

Noah looked around smiling and pointing to himself.

Elsie nodded. 'Okay, I get it. You are happy. Silly of me to assume otherwise. I mean, you do have the **greatest sister ever**, right?'

Noah slowly tilted his head side to side, pinching his lips together in a look that said 'Weeeeeeell, not exactly.' Elsie poked him gently in the ribs and the two of them hugged.

As Felix looked on, he had to admit he missed Olly. He honestly never thought that was a feeling he would feel, yet here he was.

'Ah, excuse me.'

The kids turned to see a tall woman in a top hat standing behind them.

'Sorry to interrupt. My name is Isabella d'Ambray and I manage a travelling music show called **"The Toe Tappers"**.'

Elsie gasped. 'Oh, **I love that show!** I've seen it every time it comes into town. It's wonderful!'

Isabella grinned at her. 'Well, that is excellent news as I would like to invite you to join us.'

'WHAT?' Elsie looked at Noah in disbelief. 'Me?'

'Absolutely,' said Isabella. 'I have not seen a musician engage a crowd like that in a long time. We would love to have you as part of our troupe. We pay six silver pieces a day and tour for half the year.'

Elsie's jaw dropped open. 'Six silvers a day? To play my fiddle?'

Isabella nodded. 'Plus, any extra from the audience is divided between the performers. What do you say?'

Elsie took Noah's hand. 'I don't think I can do it. I couldn't leave my brother for half the year.'

'Leave him?' Isabella looked confused. 'Why would you leave him? I want the whole troupe, dancers included. Six silver each, of course.'

Elsie and Noah grabbed each other and leapt up and down. 'You won't have to do harvest, Noah! And we can travel the country . . . **together!**'

'Is that a yes?' asked Isabella.

Elsie whipped around and stuck her hand out. 'That is a million yes-es. Yes, yes, yes.'

'And you, young man?' she asked Noah.

Noah nodded so hard he looked like one of those bobble-headed dogs that sits on a car dashboard.

'Excellent.' She turned to Felix. 'And how about you?'

Felix stopped. The excitement he felt for the siblings washed away and the realisation that he might be stuck in this strange world forever poured over him. He liked Elsie and Noah, a lot, but he wanted to go home. He missed his bedroom and his dad … and even Olly. He didn't want to be a travelling jellyfish dancer. He wanted to be an average ten-year-old in Cork Bay. But maybe that was never going to happen.

'I'm not sure,' said Felix. 'I think I need to get home.'

'Well, I'm happy to just take the two of you,' Isabelle stated, indicating towards the siblings. 'Come by my tent this afternoon to sign the paperwork. Great to have you on board!' With that, she whipped around and strode off into the crowd.

Elsie put her arm around Felix. 'I'm so sorry, Felix. It looks like everything worked out for us. Noah doesn't have to work the harvest. We get to stay together. I get to play the fiddle AND we will get paid more than we ever thought we could make. But we still don't know how to get you home. You could stay with us, you know?'

Noah nodded in agreement.

'Thanks,' said Felix. 'Really, I mean that, but I need to get home.' He turned towards the crowd, his eyes scanning the strangers dressed in clothes from another time, another world. This wasn't his home. He couldn't stay.

'Well, Mago wasn't entirely wrong,' joked Elsie. 'You certainly solved all **OUR** problems.'

Felix looked at all the people in the crowd, realising there wasn't a single familiar face. He missed familiar faces. He missed his family. 'Not really. I mean, you were hoping I'd get Noah's voice back.'

Elsie hung her head. 'Yes, but I was wrong. I just need Noah. The way he is.' Elsie took Noah's hand. 'And now we can stay together. Thanks to you.'

Noah put his hand to his chest and nodded 'thank you' to Felix.

'Well, then,' Felix said to himself, 'problem solved.'

At that moment, Felix spotted a girl. A girl who stood out from the crowd. Wait, was she wearing …

REEEEKKKKKK!

There was a sound like the rusty brakes on a metro train, a blinding flash of white light and the strong smell of singed hair.

CHAPTER 13

Horse-dung do

Felix was back in his shower, water streaming onto his head, soaking the clothes he'd borrowed from Elsie and Noah.

But wait . . . had he seen what he thought he'd seen in the town square?

A girl. With frizzy brown hair and wide dark eyes. Toothbrush in her mouth and wearing a unicorn onesie. She hadn't belonged there either.

Water continued to stream down on Felix's head.

'A **BAAAAAAA-llerina!**' cried a voice from behind the bathroom door.

Felix snapped out of his trance and quickly turned the shower off. Was that Olly? Was he home? He looked around. This was definitely his bathroom. Olly's bath toys were piled along the rim of the bath. Dad's three-hundred-year-old bathrobe hung on the door. An empty toilet roll that no one EVER replaced spun around on its holder.

HE WAS HOME!

Felix stripped off his soggy medieval outfit and shoved it into the bathroom cupboard to deal with later. He snatched his towel off the hook and wrapped it around himself, pulling the door open to reveal Olly standing there with his joke book.

'Did you hear my joke? A dancing sheep? A Baaaaa-llerina. Get it?'

Felix did get it. He beamed at his little brother and pulled him into a hug.

'**Eeeewww**, you're all wet, Felix. Lemme go!'

But Felix just squeezed him harder. 'I might never let you go again! Did you miss me?'

'Miss you?' Olly wriggled out of his grip. 'You were in the shower for like two seconds. There's no way you're even clean.'

Olly stared at Felix's head, sniffed and screwed up his nose. 'Is that horse poo in your hair? Where did **THAT** come from? Did you even wash at all?!'

Felix reached up to his hair. So it really had happened.

'You are in so much trouble,' Olly smirked. 'You know Dad always checks behind our ears. No way you're getting away with a horse-dung do!'

'Dad!' Felix ran out into the kitchen, where his dad was packing the boys' lunches. He tackled him into a hug.

'Whoa there, little man!' Dad dropped a sandwich into the lunchbox and wrapped his arm around Felix. 'That's a lot of love for this early in the morning.'

'I'm just really, **REALLY** happy to see you, Dad.'

'Aw.' Dad rubbed Felix's shoulder. 'Me too, buddy. It's been a tough ten hours without you. All that sleeping.'

Felix smiled and shoved his dad. 'I mean it. It's good to be home.'

'What do you mean "be home"?' Dad said as he continued to pack the lunches. 'Where else would you be?'

It was a really good question. 'Yeah, where else would I be?'

'Now, please go and get dressed. I cannot be late today, okay? And can you help with Olly? I know you find it the most painful punishment that an evil dad like me has ever created, but it would really help me out.'

'Of course. No problem.' Felix gave his dad a quick kiss. 'Love you, Dad.'

'Love you too, little man.'

Felix walked off towards his room but stopped at the hallway. 'Hey, Dad.'

'Yeah,' he replied, trying to make the fruit fit in the lunchbox like it was a game of Tetris.

'If you need me to help out with any more chores and stuff, I can. I'm ten now, I can do more work around here.'

Dad froze, banana still poking up from the lunchbox. 'I'm sorry, what? Are you feeling okay?'

Felix laughed. 'I mean it, Dad. I could help more.'

'Wow. Okay, I'm never going to say no to that. Thanks, Felix. That would be great.'

'No problem.' Felix smiled. 'Just stick around, okay? And don't send me to harvest.'

Dad's face crinkled. 'Send you to what?'

'Nothing.'

Dad shrugged. 'So, are we on for a movie night tonight?'

'Only if there's popcorn!' Felix walked off, calling out to his brother. '**Olly!** Are you dressed yet? Do you need help packing your school bag?'

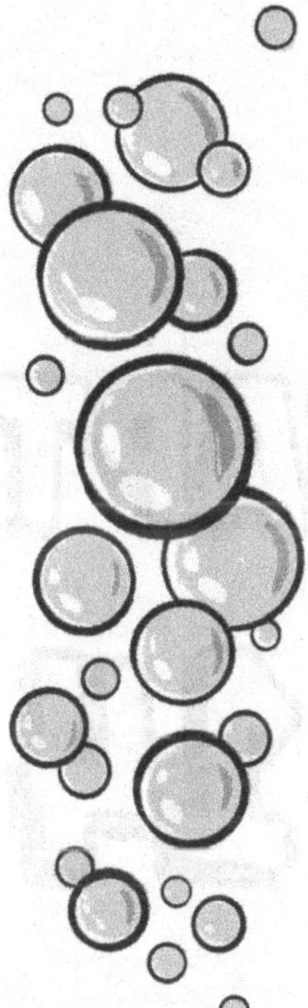

CHAPTER 14

Willing to stink

Felix sat on the school bus with Olly next to him, who was telling jokes from his book. But Felix didn't mind. To be fair, he wasn't really listening. All he could think about was the shower.

Had it really happened? Was it real? Maybe it was all just a dream. Maybe he had still been asleep from the night before. But as Felix clutched his school bag, he could feel the brown leather boots inside. If it were all a dream, then he wouldn't have an entire medieval outfit to dispose of.

Well, one thing was for sure, Felix was **NEVER** showering again. He wasn't going to risk getting stuck in another world, never to see his family. He was willing to stink if it meant staying right where he belonged.

He thought about Elsie and Noah. About witches' curses and corn gobblers and armies on the battlefield, about Mystical Mago, Noah's hilarious dance moves and the sound of Elsie's fiddle as it filled the town square with joy. But there was one thing he really couldn't stop thinking about.

The girl.

The girl in the unicorn onesie with the toothbrush.

The girl who looked like she didn't belong.

Just like Felix.

Nat and James hate writing bios. They never know what to say about themselves. So they decided to write bios for each other.

Without using Google.

This is what they came up with ...

About Nat Amoore

(By James Hart)

After finishing school, Nat Amoore ran away to join the circus. It was a fifteen-hour train ride, through snow and blizzards and hail and a plague of smelly rats, but she made it. She had dreams of becoming the world's most lovable strong-clown-tightrope walker. However, her circus career was short-lived, as no sooner had she arrived than she received a mysterious letter with a mysterious symbol upon the envelope. I'd draw it for you here, but I am, alas, restricted to typing letters into words.

Which is what Nat Amoore **IS** extremely good at. Like really, really,

REALLY good! So good, in fact, that this is the reason she received this mysterious letter. Not only was it mysterious with a mysterious symbol on it, but printed on the back in mysterious silver ink were the letters **P, T, O, C, S, E, T, R, E**. Which, when read in the correct order, made words that only a handful of skilled literary geniuses could decipher.

Not a lot is known of her life after the point at which Nat opened that letter. It is all a mysterious mystery. Some say she captained a pirate ship across the seven seas for a few years; others say she was a roadie for the most famous rock band of all time; even more say she worked as a code-breaking genius for a special government agency in Hungary.

But of all the stories that surround Nat, the one that I believe the most is her time as official head chef for the King of Siberia. Where she once cooked for three weeks straight, without eating, without sleeping and without even going to the toilet!! But the other story that I believe even more than that is that she went on to write many of her secret adventures down and make them into **wonderfully entertaining books** for kids.

Her passion for kids and reading oozes out of her like melted cheese from a freshly toasted cheese toastie. Which I'm pretty sure would be up there as her favourite food, especially after being a head chef, and all. And when she takes a bite of that toastie you will see that signature Nat Amoore smile that brightens up everyone's day.

If you want to see Nat smile and delve into her mysterious world simply ask a parent's permission (any parent will do, even mine) to drive you to her house and knock on her door. She lives somewhere in New South Wales, I think. But be warned, if you tap the wrong rhythm on her door you'd better be prepared to **RUN!!!!!!**

If you aren't a great runner or physically active at all, just do what all of us lazy people do: go on the internet and look up **natamoore.com**. You'll be happy you did!

About James Hart

(By Nat Amoore)

James Hart is a really, **REALLY** good illustrator. Before this book I already knew he was good but turns out he's next level. He has illustrated a whole bunch of books. Like **WAY** too many to list. If you wanna learn about them all, then you know how to use Google. Or, you could try **jameshart.com.au**. Most of the books he has made have been with far more impressive authors, so I feel super grateful that he lowered the bar and agreed to work with me.

I'm pretty sure he used to live in Melbourne, but rumour has it he went all Bear Grylls style and moved out to a farm somewhere. I don't know where. No one does. Don't try to find him, he doesn't want to be found. I like to imagine him happily feeding pigs and growing organic basil in between drawing pictures for Shower Land.

He has kids. I don't know how many, but I'm sure they are all **as cool as their dad**.

He probably studied something at some point, but I think any qualifications he might have are completely overshadowed by his raw natural talent.

James looks like the kind of guy who would let you push in line at the toilet if you were **REALLY** busting to pee. I reckon he is probably a coffee drinker. He used to work in animation, I think, and I've never met an animator who doesn't drink coffee. I don't reckon he's a herbal tea kinda guy. He also writes emails like he talks, all informal and funny. I love people who do that.

I saw a video of him once where he had a giant Lego man head sitting in the background. I also own one of those and that leads me to assume that we could definitely be **best friends**.

One day James and I will meet in person and maybe climb a tree together. Then I will buy him one of my favourite monster shakes and we can argue about which comic books are the best in a sunny outdoor cafe.

Felix refuses to shower. Last time, he ended up in another world. But Dad and Olly have noticed he smells pretty bad. At least he's prepared this time, wearing speedos just in case. He turns on the shower and …

REEEEKKKKKK!

Felix finds himself on a mountain … freezing … knee-deep in snow.

Step 1: **Find pants AGAIN.**

Step 2: Rescue kids from a giant **YETI.**

Step 3: **WAIT, WHAT DID YOU SAY?!?**

Felix's shower is a portal to another world. Never fear. He's ready for anything this time, with a backpack full of survival gear. He turns on the shower and …

REEEEKKKKKK!

Felix finds himself in the middle of the ocean … sinking … but there's a ship on the horizon.

Step 1: **Don't drown.**

Step 2: **Don't think about sharks.**

Step 3: **WHO IS THAT MYSTERY GIRL?**